I'm Reading About

WYOMING

The Equality State!

GALLOPADE

by Carole Marsh

Printed and Manufactured in Peachtree City, GA., USA
www.gallopade.com

Book design: John Hanson

Editorial manager: Janice Baker

Wyoming is a great state.

It is one of a kind.

What makes Wyoming special?

Let's read about it
and see!

NATIVE AMERICANS

Who lived in Wyoming first?

Native Americans did!

They moved around to find food.
They hunted for animals to eat.
They fished in Wyoming's rivers.
They gathered fruits and seeds and nuts.

EXPLORERS

The first explorer came to Wyoming in 1807.
He had been part of the Lewis and Clark Expedition.

His name was John Colter.
He traveled through the Wyoming wilderness.
He is known as a "mountain man."

HISTORY

Fort Laramie was one of the first settlements in Wyoming.
It was built where the Laramie River and North Platte River meet.

Fort Laramie was an important stop for travelers heading west on the Oregon Trail.
Pioneers stocked up on supplies at the fort!

Fort Laramie started out as a fur trading post called Fort William.

Fort Laramie

STATEHOOD

Wyoming was the 44th state
to join the United States of America!

Isn't it great,
to be a state!
I bet Wyoming
could hardly wait!

Wyoming became a state in 1890.

Wyoming

The 44th State

FLAG

I am the state flag.
I was adopted in 1917.

What colors am I?
I am red, white, and blue.

Look at me.
What else do you see?

I fly high over the state of Wyoming!

GREAT SEAL OF THE STATE OF WYOMING
EQUAL RIGHTS
LIVESTOCK
MINES
GRAIN

CAPITAL

Say hello to Cheyenne,
the capital city of Wyoming!

There is an important building in Cheyenne.
It is the State Capitol.
Wyoming's laws are made there!

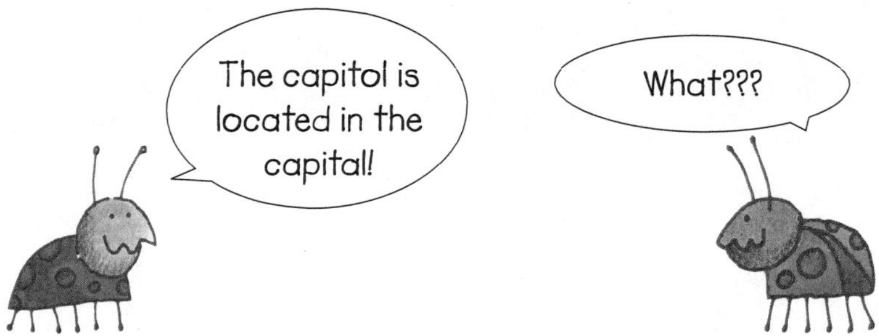

Capitol

SEAL

I am a seal,
but I am not the State Seal.
If I were, I would be very important.
I would be stamped on many official papers.
(Ouch, that might hurt!)

GREAT SEAL OF THE STATE OF WYOMING
EQUAL RIGHTS
LIVESTOCK
GRAIN
MINES
OIL
1869
1890

Now, that's official!

NICKNAME

State nicknames are fun!
State nicknames are great!
They share fun facts
about each state!

Wyoming's nickname is "The Equality State."

Wyoming was the first state to give women the right to vote!

The Equality State

BORDERS

Look at Wyoming.
Wyoming is in a region called "the West."

Wyoming borders six other states.
Find them on the map!

Wyoming has the fewest people of all 50 states.

Borders

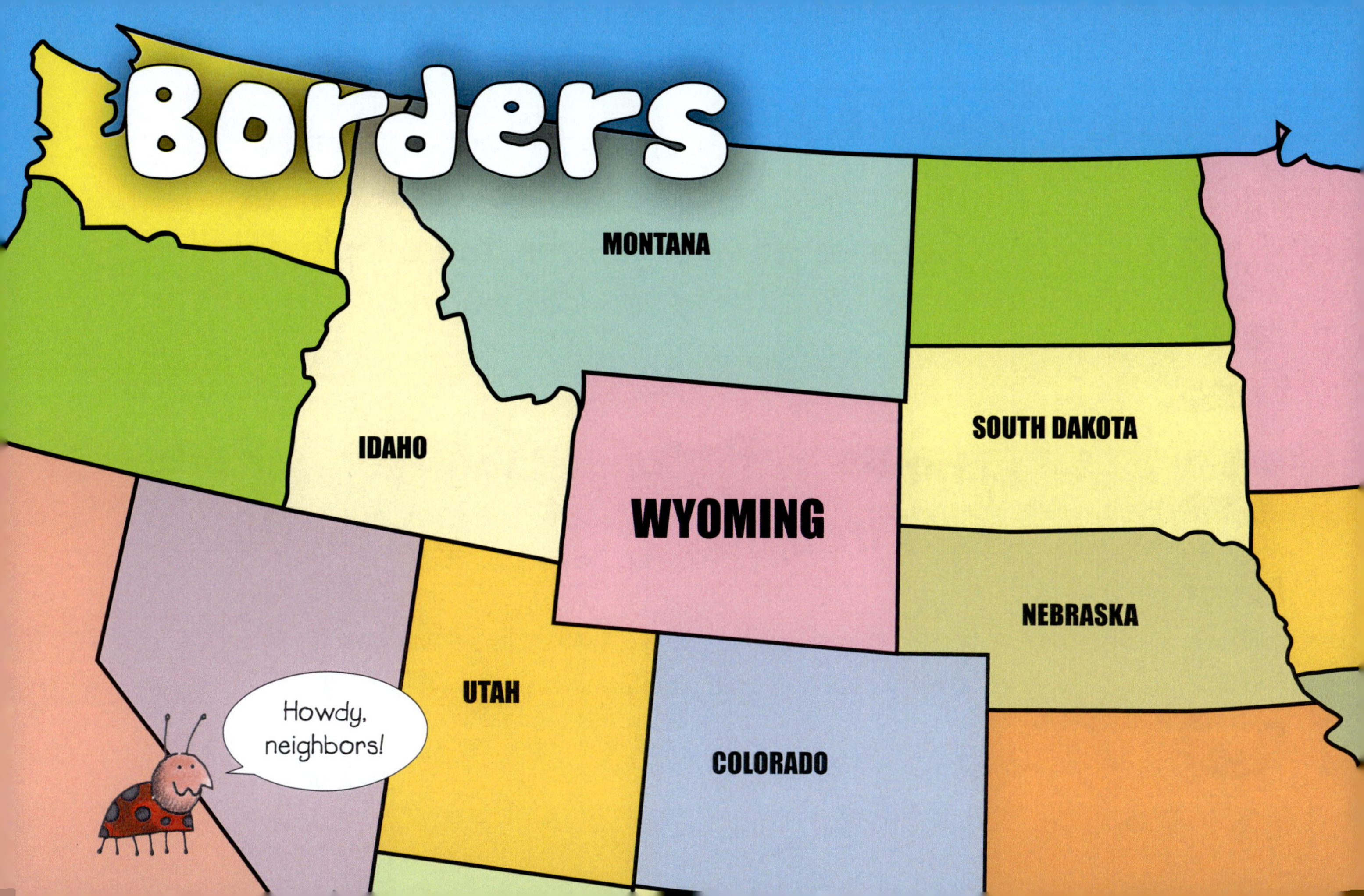
MONTANA
IDAHO
SOUTH DAKOTA
WYOMING
NEBRASKA
UTAH
COLORADO
Howdy, neighbors!

COUNTIES

Wyoming is divided into 23 counties.
Counties are a form of local government.
Counties provide services that people need!
Those services include:

Schools **Parks** **Libraries** **Police**
Firefighters **and More!**

Counties

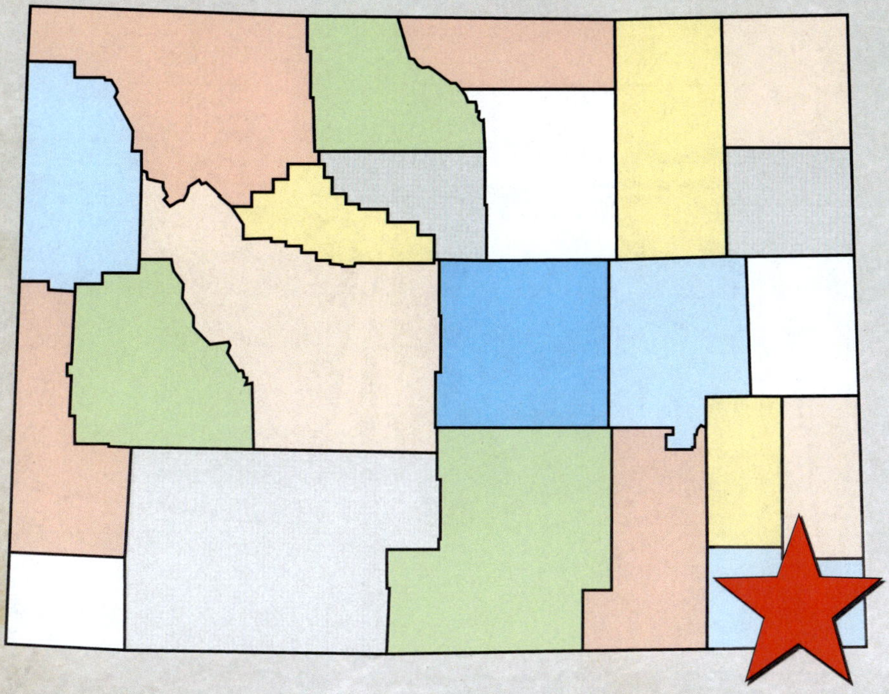

PEOPLE

Many famous people

Chief Washakie

Shoshone Indian chief

Esther Hobart Morris

First female U.S. Justice of the Peace

William "Buffalo Bill" Cody

Buffalo hunter and showman who founded Cody, Wyoming

call our state home!

Let's hang out!

Jackson Pollock

Artist known for his unique style of action painting

Patricia MacLachlan

Children's book author who wrote *Sarah, Plain and Tall*

Richard Cheney

U.S. Vice President under President George W. Bush

PEOPLE

Meadowlark

I am the state bird, and I fly
over Wyoming, proud and high.

As I fly, up in the sky,
I flap my wings to tell you "Hi!"

The Wyoming state bird is the Meadowlark.

BIRD

Indian Paintbrush

FLOWER

I am the Indian Paintbrush.
I am the state flower.

I grow where it's warm and sunny.
I bloom in spring and summer.
I help make Wyoming beautiful!

Look at me! Smell me!
I look like I have been dipped in
bright red paint.

Cottonwood

TREE

I am a Cottonwood—I'm the state tree.
All over Wyoming is where to find me.

My roots run deep, they keep me strong.
I can live 100 years—that's very long!

I stand up straight, big and tall.
Don't climb too high—it would hurt to fall!

Sheridan's Green Hairstreak Butterfly

BUTTERFLY

I am the Sheridan's Green Hairstreak Butterfly.
I am the state butterfly.

I flit and I fly from flower to flower.
I am looking for nectar to drink.

Look at my beautiful wings.
What colors do you see?

Prairie

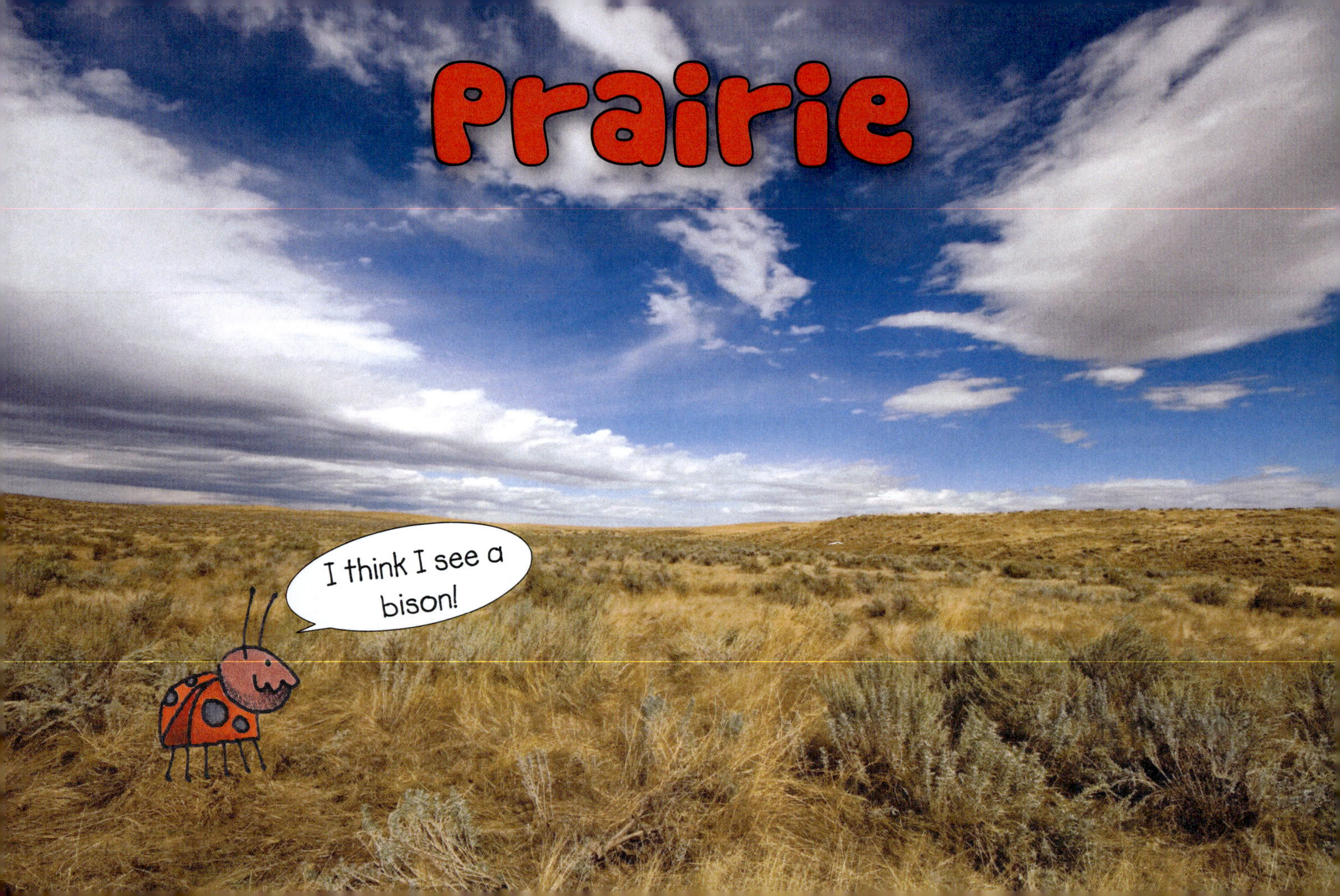

PRAIRIE

Let's go to the prairie!

Wyoming has miles of prairies.
The tall golden grass
sways in the breeze.

The prairie is flat.
There are no trees.
It stretches as far as the eye can see!

Wyoming's prairies are home to many animals:

Prairie Dogs **Badgers** **Coyotes** **Bison** **Deer** **and More!**

Rocky Mountains

MOUNTAINS

Wyoming's Rocky Mountains are the place to be.
Hiking, fishing, camping—
fun for you and me.

Winter weather brings lots of snow.
Temperatures drop to freezing and below!

Rivers

RIVERS

Wyoming has many rivers.
People like to use rivers for boating and fishing!

This habitat is home to many animals:

Birds Deer Snakes Frogs Fish and More!

The Snake River is the largest river in Wyoming.

Devils Tower

LANDMARK

Devils Tower is a giant rock!
The rock stretches high above the ground around it.

The top of Devils Tower is flat.
The tower has deep ruts up and down its sides that look like columns.

People are allowed to climb Devils Tower.
They have to register with park rangers to do it!

Wyoming Crops

AGRICULTURE

Wyoming has many farms.
Why?
Because Wyoming has good soil and a mild climate!

Some of the top crops grown in Wyoming are:

Sugarbeets **Barley** **Dry beans** **Wheat**

Sports in Wyoming

SPORTS

Baseball! Basketball! Football!
Wyoming has it all.

Whether you like to watch or play,
You are sure to have a ball!

Cowboys **Cowgirls**

Thunderbirds

Rustlers

& More!

Wyoming: Home of Yellowstone National Park

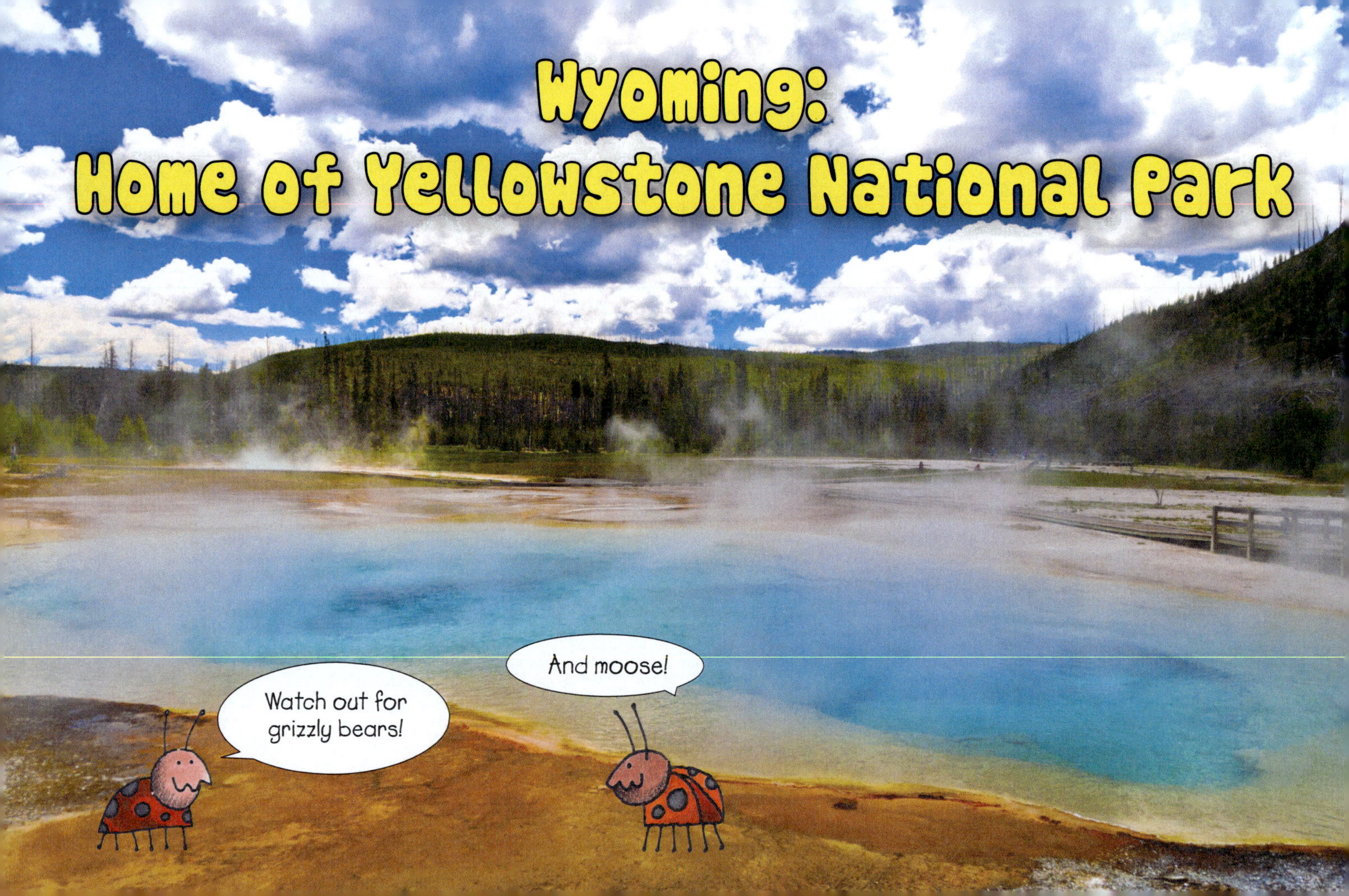

CLAIM TO FAME

Yellowstone National Park is in Wyoming!
Yellowstone has lakes, canyons, rivers, and mountains.

The most popular attraction at Yellowstone is Old Faithful!
Old Faithful is a geyser.
It spews water about every 90 minutes!

Yellowstone was the very first national park!

GLOSSARY

climate: weather conditions in an area over a long period of time

equality: when two people or things are treated the same

geyser: a hot spring that shoots water and steam into the air

habitat: a place where plants or animals naturally live

Justice of the Peace: a county judge

laws: rules made by the government

pioneer: a person who is the first to explore a new place

region: an area that has similar characteristics

settlement: the first community in an area

wilderness: a place where only wild animals live